The Bunny Br First Thanksgiving

By Dori Hoch

Illustrated by Jane Wolfgang

To Arabella
Happy Thanksgiving!
Dori Hoch
2015

Summary: Benjamin and Bobby Bunny want to celebrate Thanksgiving just like the Pilgrims and Indians did long ago. Determined to find a turkey for their feast, the brothers don their bows and arrows and go hunting. Clever Tom Turkey comes up with an idea that puts a new spin on Thanksgiving traditions.

ISBN: 978-1515037064

Printed in Charleston, SC

To Frank – my extremely patient husband
– D.H.

To Brian – Thank you for all of your love and support.
– J.W.

The chilly late autumn breeze swayed the curtains. Bobby Bunny was reading so intently that he didn't even notice that his brother was juggling his Easter Eggs.

"Hey, Benjamin, did you know that the Pilgrims came to our country on a boat called the Mayflower? They wore funny hats, hunted turkeys, and ate them on the first Thanksgiving. Wouldn't it be fun to have our very own Thanksgiving feast?"

"Now where are we going to find a turkey?" asked Benjamin.

"The Pilgrims hunted lots of them. I'll bet we can find one in our woods. Let me get my bow and arrow. I'm sure I'll get a turkey before you," said Bobby.

"No way! I'll get one first!" Benjamin boasted.

5

Off went the brothers in search of a turkey. Golden and scarlet leaves crunched under their paws as Bobby led them through the forest. Suddenly, Bobby saw something move under him.

Groundhog popped his head out of his hole. "Hey! Watch where you're stepping!"

"Sorry about that, Groundhog. Do you know where we can find a turkey?" asked Bobby. "We want one to eat for our first Thanksgiving."

"I saw something brown fly by me," said Groundhog.

"Thanks."

The brothers hiked onward.

"What are you two plump bunnies doing near my den?" asked a fox.

"Fox, do you know where we can find a turkey? We want one to eat for our first Thanksgiving," Benjamin explained.

"No, I did not see a turkey. And if I did, I would want that tasty bird for myself," he replied, licking his lips. "Go away or you will be my dinner! Can't you see I am trying to get some sleep?"

Leaving in a hurry, Bobby and Benjamin continued their search. Skunk was taking her children for a walk. "Skunk, do you know where we can find a turkey?" asked Bobby. "We want one to eat for our first Thanksgiving."

"No, I did not see a turkey. I've been strutting with my babies."

As the brothers neared a stream, they both spotted a brown bird with a colorful neck darting behind a tree. "A turkey! A turkey!" Benjamin exclaimed as he fired his bow. Down flew the arrow into a pile of leaves.

"Getting a turkey might be harder than we thought," Bobby remarked.

The brothers continued walking. "A turkey's nest!" cried Bobby. "Benjamin, go home and get a box and a stick. Bring an ear of corn, too. Turkeys love corn!"

After setting the trap, the brothers hid behind a tree. They waited and waited and waited. As day turned to night, the brothers fell fast asleep.

As the sun rose in the East, Bobby nudged his brother. "Wake up. Let's check the trap."

Bobby slowly lifted up the box, with Benjamin ready to grab the turkey. "It's empty! That bird ate the corn and left!"

"Will we ever get that turkey?" Benjamin sighed.

"Let's use one of those knots in our Bunny Scout Handbook," Bobby suggested.

The next day the brothers returned to the nest. Up went the rope over a thick oak branch. They made a loop and piled leaves over it. Then Bobby sprinkled corn on top. While hiding, Benjamin and Bobby fought over holding the rope. By and by the weary bunnies fell fast asleep.

Just as dawn was breaking, the brothers heard a loud cry. They jumped onto their paws.

"Eeek! Eeeek!   Help! Help! Help! "

"A turkey!   We got a turkey!" shouted Bobby.

Sure enough, hanging right in front of the big oak tree was a turkey, dangling by its feet.

"Let me down! What is the meaning of this?" squawked the bird.

"You're going to be our Thanksgiving turkey, just like the Pilgrims and the first Thanksgiving!" explained Benjamin.

"What? Are you crazy? You fellows are bunnies. Bunnies are vegetarians! You eat carrots, carrot stew, and carrot dumplings! Turkeys are for people, not bunnies!"

"Well... but the book says..." explained Bobby.

"Listen. I'm Tom Turkey. Let's make a deal. If you get me out of this rope, I'll share my grandmother's secret recipe. It will make your Thanksgiving feast fantastic. TRULY FANTASTIC!"

"Hi, Tom. I'm Benjamin and this is my brother, Bobby. What kind of recipe? Candied carrots? Deviled carrots? Apple carrot salad?" he guessed.

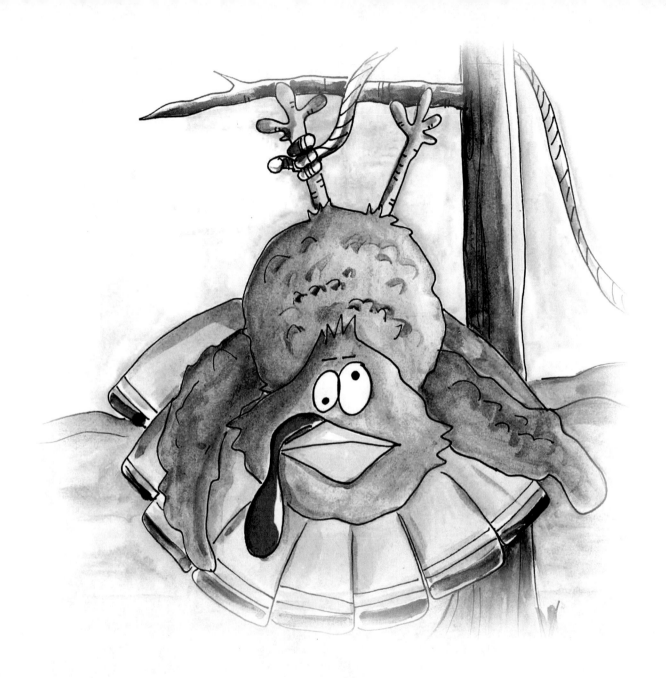

"Please, let's talk animal to animal. I'm getting dizzy!   Believe me boys, you'll be glad to change your menu when you taste my treat," Tom said.

Bobby and Benjamin stepped aside to discuss Tom's fate.
"Hmm," said Bobby.
"Hmmm," replied Benjamin.
"Hmmmm," they said.
"Let's try his recipe," decided Bobby.

23

Sadly Benjamin agreed, putting away his bow and arrow. Freeing the rope from the tree, the brothers walked side by side, pulling their new friend behind them.

The burrow became a very busy place. Bowls, spoons, flour, salt, and sugar were everywhere. Tom Turkey followed his recipe step by step. Bobby measured while Benjamin added and stirred. Some of the batter made it into the baking pan while the rest splattered all over the place.

With sweet aromas filling the burrow, Mother Rabbit joined her sons at the table.   And a special place was added for Tom Turkey right between Bobby and Benjamin.

Besides carrot juice and carrot stew, a new dish was added. "Yessiree," declared Bobby. "Tom, your secret recipe is delicious!"

"Can I have another one?" asked Benjamin.

"We've started a new tradition!" exclaimed Mother Rabbit. "From now on, we'll make Tom Turkey's carrot muffins for our feast. And Tom, you will always be our guest. What a great way to celebrate our first Thanksgiving!"

"Yes, indeed, this truly is a day to be thankful," gobbled Tom with a huge, toothless smile. "A mighty wonderful tradition indeed!"

Tom Turkey's Carrot Muffins

Ingredients

1 ½ c. flour
¾ c. sugar
1 tsp. baking soda
½ tsp. salt
1/3 c. salad oil
1 T. vinegar
1 tsp. vanilla
1 c. grated carrots
1 tsp. cinnamon
1 c. cold water

Directions

1. Heat oven to 350 degrees F
2. Spray the bottom and sides of mini-muffin pan with cooking spray or use paper liners
3. Mix flour, sugar, baking soda and salt together
4. Add the rest of the ingredients, stirring until well mixed
5. Pour into cups of mini-muffin pan
6. Bake 20 minutes or until golden brown and toothpick inserted in center comes out clean
7. Makes about 36 mini-muffins

Cream Cheese Icing

4 oz. cream cheese
¼ c. of butter or margarine
½ lb. box 10x sugar
1 tsp. vanilla

With cream cheese and margarine/butter at room temperature, mix with electric mixer until blended. Slowly add confectioners' sugar and vanilla. Spread icing on cooled muffins and refrigerate.

24794919R00020

Made in the USA
Middletown, DE
07 October 2015